A JOURNEY THROUGH TIME

SUSHRUT KUMAR PATRALEKH

Copyright © Sushrut Kumar Patralekh
All Rights Reserved.

ISBN 979-888546438-3

Contents

Preface

Fagertin was normal man untill he started traveling through time. The book is about his story, he goes on many adventures and along the way makes some friends. Join him on his journey through time!

Volume 1

ONE

A NORMAL LIFE

"Ok ok, fine I'll teach you history." said Fagertin with a small amount of fear. His son then shouted, "YAY!" The scream was so loud that his wife screamed at him for supposedly making their son sad. Fagertin had to then go to work and sell pasta. He was living a very normal life for a thirty-six year old. He didn't want anything to change; he was happy with the life he had. His son was nine years old and he lived with both his parents. Fagertin while at work found some sort of strange stick. He then touched the top of the stick and suddenly he was teleported to the time realm.

TWO
MANY DIFFERENT YEARS

Fagertin was very confused about where he was. The time realm held the information of everything that had has and will happen. Because Fagertin studied a lot of languages he was easily able to read the messages on the sort of walls in the time realm. It looked like some sort of middle dimension. It had a circular wall like a hamster wheel that extend so long that it would take over ten hundred trillion years to get to the end of it. There were many circular portals that were purple in colour. Soon Fagertin realized that all the history books were very wrong. Fagertin went through many different years, studying about how history actually went down. He wrote all of his discovery's in two copies. The first one he planned to bring back to his time to teach his son real history. The other one he planned to bury it somewhere during the iron age so that hopefully archaeologists would study his version of history instead of the fake ones. But the main event happened in 1349. When he went to that year he spawned in a cave. He explored for some time and eventually he realized that he was in the middle of the black death. He checked where he was in his phone and realized he was in the area that would in the future become his house. He went ahead and created a portal to the time dimension because he didn't want to get infected. But when he opened the portal a rampaging lion jumped through the portal. And went into the time realm. Fagertin jumped through the portal to chase the lion. The lion bit a wall of the time realm and a giant shock wave glitched time itself. Fagertin's right hand turned into a lion's face. Suddenly the item that would explode into the big bang appeared and started exploding. Suddenly an army of agents paused the big bang and pushed it back to the time where it came from and unpaused it and closed the portal. Fagertin then went to the year 300 bc and put one of his two copies in the dirt. Suddenly a few of the same agents came and said, "Your coming with us." they then took Fagertin to some sort of court room.

THREE
THE TIME COURT

Fagertin went into the court room and screamed, "I SWEAR, I DIDN'T STEAL THE COPIES!".

"This isn't about the copies Fagertin Garafi." said one of the agents to Fagertin. Then the judge said, "But it is about what you where about to do with them. If archaeologists discovered your book then they would print another book explaining real history thus making it so that you never would have put the copy there in the first place. This is what we as the time officers try to prevent. If you would have put the copy there then it would create a gractamoli.", "You mean paradox right? Oh this reminds me of a show called lo-" suddenly one of the agents said, "Do not talk if not needed.","Ok." said Fagertin in response. The judge then said, "A gractamoli is an event that will lead to the destruction of all of the universe and the body that inhabits them."The judge paused for a second and said, "If you did that it would lead to your and all of our deaths!" The judge stayed silent. Fagertin then responded, "Ok I just won't put the copy there and everything will be fine ok?","Are you serious!" shouted the judge. "Almost causing an event like that is unacceptable! You almost caused trillions of octillons of deaths! You are a fool to think just saying I won't do it can solve this! The worst way that we can punish someone is to erase that person's memory and even that is not enough to finish your punishment!" Fagertin at that point was very scared for his life. The judge then got out of his chair and started kicking Fagertin. "So this is how it's gonna go isn't it?" Fagertin then started attacking the judge with his chops jumps kicks and punches. Soon the judge was bleeding all over. The judge then cried, "Please spare my life I beg you." The judge then turned into his true form, a god. The judge then said, "Hello Fagertin Garafi, I am Manaik the god of stupidity. I am also the son of Mariana the goddess of time." Fagertin then responded with, "So are you very stupid or what?", Manik then said,"No. I can sense if anyone is doing something stupid and if he or she is stupid themselves." Fagertin then responded saying, "So why are you the judge of the time court thing? I mean your mom is the god of time. Shouldn't she be running this place?", "That's where you are wrong." said Manik. "You see one day around sixteen thousand years ago I was with my mother watching her watch time. I decided to use my idiot sensing power because I was quite bored. I realized that how she was governing the time realm and all of time itself was horrible. So I formed this time court to punish those who have caused a crime in time. The most common one being mass genocide." Fagertin then responded with, "So what are you going to do to me?" Manik then said in response, "Fine I will allow you to keep your life and memory but you cannot put that book there nor teach your son what you have learned. Do you understand?" Fagertin then replied with, "I understand.", "So go now! Back to your family! Just as I probably should as well.", Fagertin then said, "Nice I can go back home now!" Fagertin made a portal back to the time realm and started searching for his time portal, but then something strange happened.

FOUR

THE FLOOD OF FAGERTINS

Suddenly a bunch of Fagertins came out of the portal saying, "Where am I?" Suddenly another army of agents came to kill the extra Fagertins. "Everyone, attack!", screamed the general. Suddenly all of agents ran at the Fagertins and started shooting them with their guns. One of the agents dropped their gun so Fagertin picked it up and started destroying clones of himself. But it wasen't enough. Suddenly Manik and Mariana showed up and said,"Don't worry we'll take care of this." Suddenly they started putting some dust on the copies of Fagertin. All the Fagertins disapper after the dust was put one them. But then suddenly on of the agents thought that Fagertin was one of the clones of himself and put some of the dust on him too. Suddenly Fagertin started to fade. "FAGERTIN!", Shouted Manik and Mariana. Manik took Fagertin in his hand and said," Oh no! You were hit by disser dust! We need to get you to the beach of life, and quick! You aren't a clone of, well yourself so the disser dust's effects are for now paused. Now lets stop talking and get him to the beach!" Fagertin then turned slightly transparent. He was fading quickly.

FIVE

FINDING THE BEACH

They immediately went to the year thirty thousand and sixteen and they saw a kid who was going to infinity land with a cyborg. Although that was very strange they ignored it. They sprinted to a random person, Manik then asked, "In which direction is the beach of life?" the person then responded saying, "Oh that its in the north but only people who are not greedy can enter. "Ok, thanks bye!", said Mariana to the man. They sprinted north for thirty minuets but no sign of the beach of life. Suddenly a guard looked at Manik and said, "HEY YOUR THE DUPLICATER!" suddenly the guard started attacking them. Mariana was able to turn the guard back into a baby so that they could pass. After two more hours of running they finally reached the beach of life. At this point Fagertin had almost faded. They tried to go in but there was an invisible wall blocking the way. Suddenly a different guard showed up and said, "Hey only the worthy can enter this beach!" Suddenly the guard started attacking them. Mariana couldn't turn him into a baby because she was very weak after running so much. Manik used his kicks to hurt the guard a little bit. But the guard hit back hard. He punched Manik in his face and kicked him in his belly and his eye. Despite this Manik stood up ready for more. The guard then stopped fighting and said, "You are fighting so much even if you get hurt and you are doing it all for your friend. You are worthy you may pass." and so the invisible wall went away. They went into the beach of life and Fagertin was suddenly healed. Mariana then opened a portal to Fagertin's time and shouted, "GO NOW!" Fagertin jumped through the portal and he was teleported to the restaurant that he worked at. But there was another Fagertin there.

SIX

THE DUPLICATOR

Fagertin was shocked. He thought that he was not a clone, he thought that he was the original himself, but now he saw himself right in the eyes. Fagertin was shocked, he thought, "I am not my real self?! How, this can't be right! Wait! The glitter, it didn't make me vanish. Wait but then who is he?" Fagertin thought all of this in one second. He then screamed at the person who looked like him, "HEY! WHO ARE YOU AND WHY DO WANT TO LOOK LIKE ME!" the person looked at Fagertin with a grin and said, "You'll never catch me I'm The duplicator man!" Fagertin then respond saying, "That's a stupid name!" both of them then jumped out of the building through an open window. Fagertin then started looking around for the duplicator. He saw his friend Sprivy at the shop that was nearby. Suddenly another Sprivy jumped in front of him, but the other Sprivy was still at the shop. Fagertin knew that this was the duplicator. Fagertin attacked The duplicator and started kicking and punching him. Fagertin got the first punch but was quickly hurt by the duplicator's kick. He then proceeded to kick Fagertin in the legs hands and face multiple times. Fagertin then punched and kicked back. He then stole the duplicator gun and then turn The duplicator into a rock. The duplicator was now harmless. Fagertin destroyed the gun by smashing it on the floor. Fagertin then returned home from work. His wife asked, "You came home a lot earlier then normal. What's up with that?" Fagertin's child was very exited. He shouted, "DADDY TEACH ME HISTORY!" Fagertin then responded with, "Ok grab your book and lets get started."